MARGRET & H.A.REY'S
Curious George
Visits the Zoo

Adapted from the Curious George film series
edited by Margret Rey and Alan J. Shalleck

Houghton Mifflin Harcourt
Boston New York

For information about permission to reproduce selections from this book, write to:
Permissions
Houghton Mifflin Harcourt
215 Park Avenue South
New York, NY 10003

www.hmhco.com

This special edition was printed for Kohl's Department Stores, Inc. (for distribution on behalf of
Kohl's Cares, LLC, its wholly owned subsidiary) by Houghton Mifflin Harcourt.

ISBN: 978-0-544-14953-3

Manufactured in China
SCP 10 9 8 7 6 5 4 3 2 1
4500400578

Kohl's
Style #: 978-0-544-14953-3
Factory #: 123386
Manufactured Date: 5/13

This is George.

George was a good little monkey and always very curious.

One day, George's friend, the man with the yellow hat, said,
"How would you like to see a real elephant, George? Let's go to the zoo."

There was a lot to see at the zoo.

There were the giraffes with necks so long
they seemed to reach the sky,

and the kangaroos carrying their babies in special pockets.

And finally, there were the elephants with their floppy
ears and their long trunks, munching on hay.
It was lunchtime, and George was starting to feel hungry.

He saw people enjoying their lunches on park benches,

and others picnicking on the grass.

"I am going to find out what time they feed the lions,"
said the man with the yellow hat. "Please wait here and try not to get
into any trouble, George."

While George was waiting, he saw a zookeeper with a
pail of bananas for the monkeys.

The keeper put the pail down to get a drink at the water fountain.
George was hungry, so he grabbed the pail and ran away with it.

"Hey!" shouted the keeper. "Stop that monkey!"
But George kept on running.

There was a crowd of people standing near the monkey house.
This would be just the place for George to hide.

Standing by the cage was a little boy holding a red balloon with a long string. All of a sudden, one of the monkeys reached out and snatched the string from the boy's hand.

The monkey took off with the balloon and climbed to the top of the cage.

But when he tried to squeeze the balloon through the bars,
it was too big, and the other monkeys started to shriek and scream.

The little boy started to cry. "Please, can somebody get
his balloon back?" asked the mother. But none of the people
could reach that high.

George knew what to do! With the pail in his hand,
he climbed up to the top of the cage.

He took a few bananas and fed them to the monkeys.

While the monkeys were eating, George snatched the
balloon and swung down from the cage.

He handed the balloon back to the boy.

Just then the man with the yellow hat came running.
"George!" the man cried. "I have been looking all over for you!"
"Please don't be angry with him," said the mother.
"He saved my son's balloon."

23

George had saved the day! But he was still very hungry.
"Now it's time to feed ourselves, George," said the man.
And that's what they did.